The BIGGEST LITTLE BROTHER

WRITTEN BY AMINATA JALLOH   ILLUSTRATED BY KIM SPONAUGLE

To those who courageously live life with their heart.

To Alim.

Sowa's mom only made doughnuts when a special person was coming to visit.

"I can teach Hindo when he gets here," Sowa said as he cracked an egg into the bowl of batter.

Hindo was Sowa's brother. He was born in Sierra Leone and lived there with their grandmother.

Every Saturday, Sowa would sit in the living room with his mom, dad and little sister, Naiya, to video chat with Hindo.

This was Sowa's favorite time.

He would tell Hindo all about his neighborhood in Atlanta and the park he played at during the weekends.

But this Saturday was different!

Sowa's mom looked down at the bowl of doughnut batter. "Can you be a big boy and check on Dad?" she said, fishing out the bits of eggshell that Sowa had let fall into the batter.

Sowa's dad was working on the old piano in the living room.

"I can help!" Sowa shouted as he plopped onto the piano bench.

"Okay, Sowa. When I say, 'now,' press a—"

Ziiiiiiiiiiiing! Zink! Dooooooooooooonk! Sowa ran his hands across the keyboard.

"I pressed a key," Sowa sang.

Sowa's dad laughed.

"You know what—why don't you be a good big brother and make sure your sister is okay," he said, patting Sowa on the back.

Sowa hopped off the piano bench and wandered off to the bedroom he shared with Naiya.

8

"Do you want to play?" Naiya asked.

Sowa looked at the pile of dolls on the floor. One of the dolls' heads had fallen off its body.

9

"I can save you, Dolly!" Sowa shouted. Snatching the doll and its head from the floor, he popped the head back onto the body. "There! It's fixed," Sowa said triumphantly as he tossed the doll back to Naiya.

"Wait!" Naiya called out, but Sowa had already walked off.

In the living room, Sowa's dad was wiping down the piano.

"Is it time to pick up Hindo?" Sowa asked, hopping from one foot to the other.

"Yes, Sowa! You are such a big boy to remind me!"

Sowa nodded. He straightened his shoulders and stood taller. "I *am* a big boy!"

In the car, all Sowa could think about was meeting Hindo. "When Hindo gets here, I will teach him everything I know, like how to make doughnuts, how to fix things and how to play soccer." Sowa smiled as he looked out the window.

"Did you know that in Sierra Leone soccer is called *football*?" Sowa's dad said.

"Really?" Sowa asked.

"Yes! Sierra Leone is very different from America, so you will have a lot to teach Hindo just like you do with Naiya," Sowa's mom answered.

12

"Mom, will Hindo be my big brother?" Naiya
interrupted.

Sowa jumped in his seat. "No—I'm your big
brother!"

Sowa's mom turned around. "Stop it, Sowa. You
are still a big brother. But remember, now you will
also be in the middle. Isn't that special?" she said.

Sowa squirmed in his seat. That did not sound
very special.

At the airport, Hindo waved eagerly to everyone. Everyone waved back.

Everyone but Sowa.

"Hindo is such a big boy flying alone. He did not even want help carrying his bag," the airport assistant said.

"In Sierra Leone, Granny would always let me go to the market to buy fruit, and I would carry it to the house by myself," Hindo explained.

Sowa frowned.

"I can carry your bag, Hindo!" Sowa said, snatching Hindo's bag from his hand and causing it to fall to the floor with a loud thud.

"Sowa!" shouted his mom and dad.

Hindo smiled. "No problem, Sowa. I've got it." He picked up the bag. "That's what big brothers are for!"

Sowa scowled.

In the car, all Sowa could think about was how *he* used to be the big
brother.

18

When they arrived home, Sowa went straight to the kitchen.

"Hindo, I helped Mom make these doughnuts for you!" he announced in his biggest voice.

Hindo grabbed one, took a big bite and began to cough.

"I think you left an eggshell in this one," Hindo said playfully.

Everyone laughed.

Everyone except Sowa.

When dinner was served, Sowa could barely eat. He had no appetite for the jollof rice or plantains his mom had made.

After dinner, Sowa walked over to the piano and sat on the bench.

"I have always wanted to play the piano," Hindo said behind him.

"I have been trying to tune it all day," their dad said, "but I just can't seem to get the keys to hit the right notes."

"I can help!" Hindo offered—and, just like that, they set to work.

Sowa jumped off the piano bench. "I'm going to my room," he grunted, but no one was listening.

Soon, the sweet melody of the piano filled the house. Sowa pulled the sheets over his head.

I always help Dad, he thought.

23

The sound of Hindo's voice interrupted Sowa's thoughts.

"Who's that?" Hindo asked.

Sowa peered from under the covers. Naiya was holding the doll Sowa had fixed.

"She's Khadija, but her head is broken," Naiya explained.

24

Hindo took the doll from Naiya's hands. "I can fix her," he said. He wiggled the head until it snapped into place.

"Yay!" Naiya squealed. "You are the bestest big brother!" she said, giving Hindo a hug.

Sowa rolled over and pulled the sheets over his head.

"Hi," Hindo said as he seated himself at the edge of Sowa's bed.

Sowa moaned.

"I was thinking," Hindo started, "I am new to America, and I will need a lot of help figuring things out. Can you help me?"

Sowa pulled the sheets from over his head and looked at Hindo.
"You're the big brother now. I can't show you anything. I'm little."

"Hmmm . . . well, how about this? You can be the biggest little brother."

Sowa sat up. "Really?"

"Really!" Hindo said.

Sowa jumped out of bed. "I have an idea! How about I teach you to play the piano?"

"Deal!" Hindo said, following Sowa into the living room.

Sowa and Hindo sat on the piano bench, and Sowa began: *zing, zink, dong!*

The piano keys screeched under Sowa's fingers.

Hindo watched Sowa and repeated: *zing, zink, dong!*

Mom walked up to the piano, rubbing her ears. "And tomorrow, you can show Hindo the neighborhood."

Sowa put his arm around Hindo's shoulders. "Yes, I can even show you where I play soccer in the park."

Hindo tilted his head, "What's soccer?"

Sowa sat up tall and in his biggest voice said, "It is football!"

Hindo smiled. "I'd like that," he said.

Then Hindo, the big brother, and Sowa, the biggest little brother, continued to play the piano, together.

Made in the USA
Middletown, DE
02 January 2018